AN ELGAR CLARINET ALBUM

arranged by Sidney Lawton

Order No: NOV 12051601

NOVELLO PUBLISHING LIMITED

CONTENTS

*Used by permission of Schott & Co. Ltd.

Preface

For a composer of Elgar's stature, and particularly with his own keen
personal interest in wind instruments, to have left no known works,
large or small, for the clarinet, may be reckoned a matter for much
regret. Indeed, had he known that the popularity of the clarinet was
to exceed that of the violin in the second half of this century, he would
no doubt have provided as richly for the former as for the latter. This
then is the 'raison d'être' for this present album of arrangements — to
fill an unacceptable gap in the repertoire of the clarinet, and to
introduce some of the most beautiful and best-loved of Elgar's melodies
to the many thousands of clarinettists now in existence.

S.L.

AN ELGAR CLARINET ALBUM

Arranged by
SIDNEY LAWTON

SALUT D'AMOUR
Opus 12

Cat. No. 12 0516 01 01

CLARINET in Bb

CHANSON DE MATIN

Opus 15, No. 2

CHANSON DE NUIT
Opus 15, No. 1

CLARINET in B♭

ADAGIO
from the Cello Concerto
Opus 85

THEME AND VARIATION I
from 'Enigma Variations'
Opus 36

CLARINET in B♭

VARIATION XII

(B.G.N.)

from 'Enigma Variations'

Opus 36

AN ELGAR CLARINET ALBUM

Arranged by
SIDNEY LAWTON

SALUT D'AMOUR
Opus 12

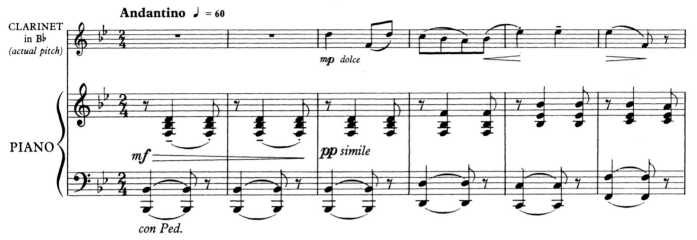

Salut D'Amour copyright Schott & Co Ltd
arrangement for clarinet and piano published by permission

CHANSON DE MATIN

Opus 15, No. 2

CHANSON DE NUIT

Opus 15, No. 1

ADAGIO
from the Cello Concerto
Opus 85

THEME AND VARIATION I
from 'Enigma Variations'
Opus 36

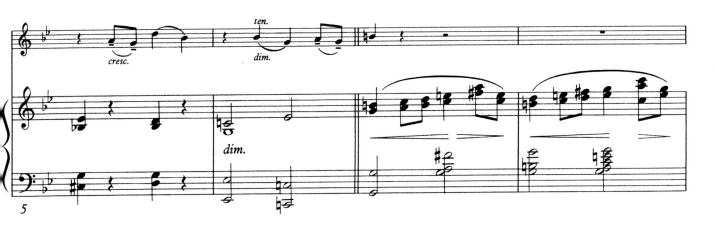

VARIATION XII
(B.G.N.)
from 'Enigma Variations'
Opus 36